Grafton Books
A Division of the Collins Publishing Group
8 Grafton Street, London W1X 3LA

Published by Grafton Books 1986

A TEMPLAR BOOK
Devised and produced by Templar Publishing
Old King's Head Court, Dorking, Surrey RH4 1AR

Illustrations copyright © 1986 by Templar Publishing Ltd
Text copyright © 1986 by Deborah Savage

Savage, Deborah
    Funny Face.— (The Adventures of Peregrine Piecrust; v.5)
    I. Title II. Forsey, Chris III. Series
    823'.914 [J] PZ7

ISBN 0-246-13004-0

Origination by Positive Colour Ltd, Maldon, Essex
Printed and bound in Great Britain by Purnell and Sons
(Book Production) Ltd, Paulton, Bristol. Member of BPCC plc

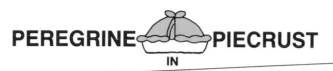

PEREGRINE PIECRUST

IN

FUNNY FACE

Written by Deborah Savage
Illustrated by Chris Forsey

GRAFTON BOOKS

A Division of the Collins Publishing Group

LONDON GLASGOW
TORONTO SYDNEY AUCKLAND

Peregrine Piecrust loved pulling faces.

His mother had invited the next-door neighbours round for tea and Peregrine had spent the whole afternoon pulling faces at them.

Unfortunately, Mrs Piecrust had seen him.

"I saw you pulling faces at the Snippets this afternoon, Peregrine," she said after they had left. "You may think it's very clever, but one of these days the wind will change direction and you'll be stuck with a funny face for ever!"

Peregrine looked at himself in the mirror and laughed.

"What nonsense," he thought, as he smoothed down his hair. "I may pull faces now and again, but the rest of the time I'm definitely still the best-looking boy in the neighbourhood!"

And he went off to look for his sister Poppy, so he could try out some of his new, most frightening faces on her.

Despite his mother's warning, Peregrine carried on pulling faces at every opportunity.

He did it at school when the teacher's back was turned. But unfortunately, the whole class burst out laughing which made Miss Prim very cross indeed.

"Now you can all stay behind and do some extra sums at breaktime," she said sternly.

But Peregrine didn't care.

On the way home he went into the greengrocer's with his mother to buy some cabbage.

First, he pulled some faces at himself in the mirror behind the counter.

Then, when he thought no-one was watching, he made himself look so ugly that the shop's cat ran away in fright and was never seen again!

Peregrine WAS enjoying himself!

And so it went on.

Whenever he could, Peregrine would stretch and twist and screw up his face into the most horrible expressions. Even though he was told time and time again not to.

Then, one blustery autumn day, Peregrine noticed Mr Prodd the policeman walking along the road outside his house.

Peregrine couldn't believe his luck!

He had just poked out his tongue and pulled one of his silliest faces when…

SOMETHING DREADFUL HAPPENED!

The wind suddenly changed direction...

And Peregrine was stuck with the most absurd expression on his face.

He had a thumb stuck in each ear, his tongue was poking out, and his eyes had

gone all round and funny.

Try as he might, Peregrine could not make his face return to normal. And when he looked in the mirror he could see that he looked very stupid indeed!

Peregrine managed to open the bedroom door with his elbows and went downstairs to the kitchen.

"Peregrine!" cried his mother when she saw him. "I told you this would happen if you carried on pulling faces at people. Now look at the mess you're in."

Just then Poppy came in from the garden.

"Oh Peregrine!" she gasped. "You won't be able to eat your tea with your tongue poking out like that! And it's jelly for pudding today!"

Peregrine was furious! Jelly was his favourite.

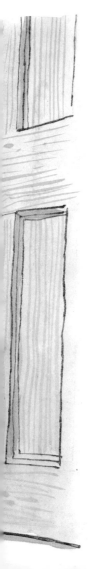

Then Mrs Piecrust had an idea.

"Poppy, I want you to go and gather together as many neighbours as you can and bring them all back here," she said.

Neither Poppy nor Peregrine had any idea what their mother was up to, but Poppy did as she was told.

Within half an hour there were about forty people in the Piecrusts' kitchen.

Mrs Piecrust clapped her hands. and asked for silence.

"I think all of you can probably guess what has happened to Peregrine," she said, and a ripple of laughter ran round the crowd.

Peregrine felt very embarrassed.

"Now, if he promises never to pull faces at anyone again, will you all help him to get back to normal?"

Peregrine made some funny grunting noises and the crowd nodded.

"Right then," said Mrs Piecrust, "on the count of three, I want everyone to blow at Peregrine as hard as they can."

"One! Two! Three! BLOW!"

A great wind filled the kitchen as everyone blew at Peregrine as hard as they could.

On the first puff, his thumbs came unstuck.

On the second puff his tongue shot back into his mouth with a snap.

And on the third puff his eyes returned to their normal size and shape so that he looked quite normal again.

Normal for Peregrine, that is!

Well, after that, Peregrine never,
ever pulled faces again.

He didn't even pull faces at
himself in the mirror just in case
there was a slight breeze. And he
took great care not to screw his
face up too much if he had an itchy
nose or anything like that.

Well, for a while anyway…